This Walker book belongs to:

_____

_____

_____

For Geraldine, Joe,
Naomi,
Eddie, Laura and Isaac
M.R.

For Amelia
H.O.

Hello Edward
Michael Rosen
was
here

Best wishes from
Helen Oxenbury.

First published 1989 by Walker Books Ltd
87 Vauxhall Walk, London SE11 5HJ

This edition published 2014

10 9 8 7 6 5 4 3 2 1

Text © 1989 Michael Rosen
Illustrations © 1989 Helen Oxenbury

The right of Michael Rosen and Helen Oxenbury
to be identified as author and illustrator respectively
of this work has been asserted by them in accordance
with the Copyright, Designs and Patents Act 1988

This book has been typeset in Veronan Light Educational

Printed in China

British Library Cataloguing in Publication Data:
a catalogue record for this book is available from
the British Library

ISBN: 978-1-4063-5296-2

www.walker.co.uk

We're Going on a Bear Hunt

25TH ANNIVERSARY EDITION

Retold by
Michael Rosen

Illustrated by
Helen Oxenbury

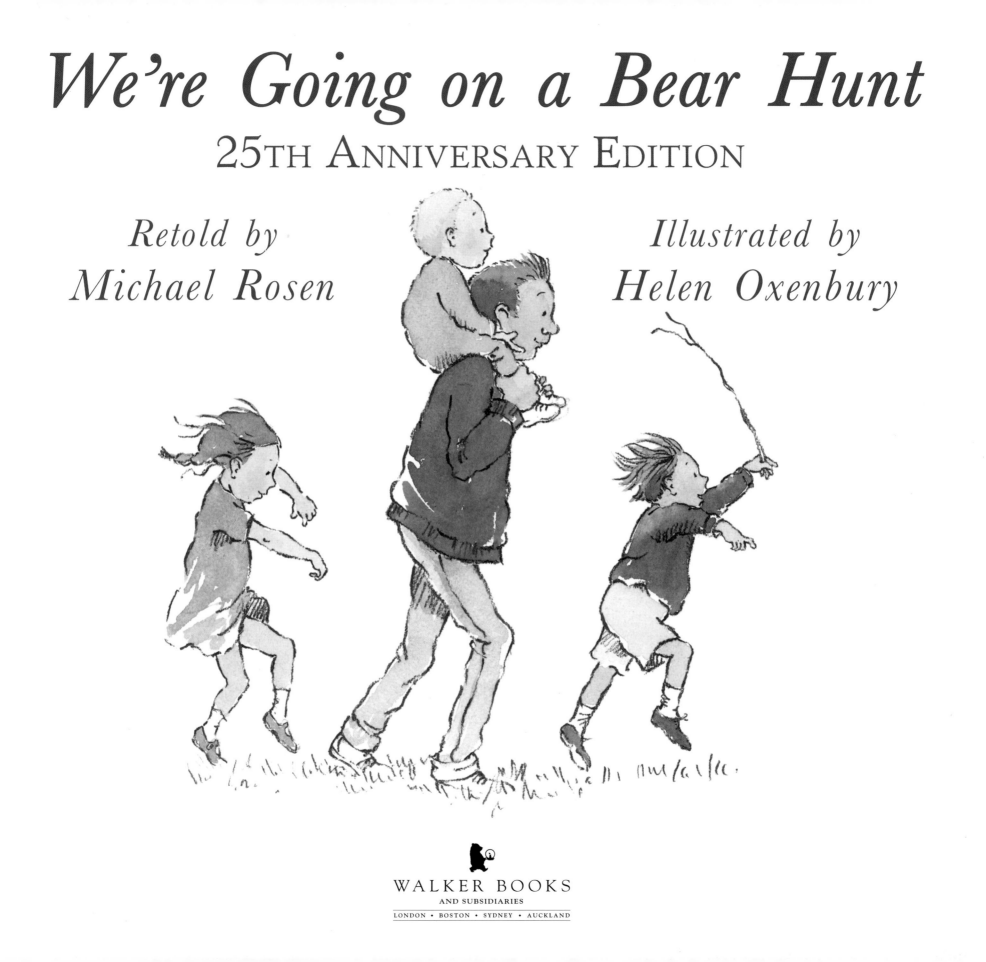

WALKER BOOKS

AND SUBSIDIARIES

LONDON · BOSTON · SYDNEY · AUCKLAND

We're going on a bear hunt.

We're going to catch a big one.

What a beautiful day!

We're not scared.

Uh-uh! Grass!

Long wavy grass.

We can't go over it.

We can't go under it.

Oh no!

We've got to go through it!

Swishy swashy!
Swishy swashy!
Swishy swashy!

We're going on a bear hunt.

We're going to catch a big one.

What a beautiful day!

We're not scared.

Uh-uh! A river!
A deep cold river.
We can't go over it.
We can't go under it.

Oh no!
We've got to go through it!

Splash splosh!
Splash splosh!
Splash splosh!

We're going on a bear hunt.

We're going to catch a big one.

What a beautiful day!

We're not scared.

Uh-uh! Mud!

Thick oozy mud.

We can't go over it.

We can't go under it.

Oh no!

We've got to go through it!

Squelch squerch!
Squelch squerch!
Squelch squerch!

We're going on a bear hunt.

We're going to catch a big one.

What a beautiful day!

We're not scared.

Uh-uh! A forest!

A big dark forest.

We can't go over it.

We can't go under it.

Oh no!

We've got to go through it!

Stumble trip!
Stumble trip!
Stumble trip!

We're going on a bear hunt.

We're going to catch a big one.

What a beautiful day!

We're not scared.

Uh-uh! A snowstorm!
A swirling whirling snowstorm.
We can't go over it.
We can't go under it.

Oh no!
We've got to go through it!

Hoooo woooo!
Hoooo woooo!
Hoooo woooo!

We're going on a bear hunt.

We're going to catch a big one.

What a beautiful day!

We're not scared.

Uh-uh! A cave!

A narrow gloomy cave.

We can't go over it.

We can't go under it.

Oh no!

We've got to go through it!

Tiptoe!

Tiptoe!

Tiptoe!

WHAT'S THAT?

One shiny wet nose!

Two big furry ears!

Two big goggly eyes!

IT'S A BEAR!!!!

Quick! Back through the cave! Tiptoe! Tiptoe! Tiptoe!

Back through the snowstorm! Hoooo wooooo! Hoooo wooooo!

Back through the forest! Stumble trip! Stumble trip! Stumble trip!

Back through the mud! Squelch squerch! Squelch squerch!

Back through the river! Splash splosh! Splash splosh! Splash splosh!

Back through the grass! Swishy swashy! Swishy swashy!

Get to our front door.

Open the door.

Up the stairs.

Oh no!

We forgot to shut the door.

Back downstairs.

Shut the door.

Back upstairs.

Into the bedroom.

Into bed.

Under the covers.

We're not going on

a bear hunt again.

"I'm always amazed and delighted by 'Bear Hunt'. I learnt it in the
early eighties as a song for children to join in with. It's a chant, a poem,
a fun-and-games romp with actions to make up and moments of shock
and horror to giggle over. When I was asked to turn it into a story
to be illustrated, I wondered if it was possible but I had a try, added
some words of my own and waited. Then came the day I saw
Helen Oxenbury's pictures – and I was utterly blown away. She had
turned those words into a family epic: a set of difficulties that a father
and his children face together in a landscape of depth, beauty
and emotion. And when you look into the book, there are powerful
feelings to explore: fear, worry, exultation and sympathy.
After all, what is the bear thinking on the last page?"

Michael Rosen